# THE GIRL
*Who Lost*
# EVERYTHING

# THE GIRL
## *Who Lost*
# EVERYTHING

# Siobhan Addo-yeboah

Order this book online at www.trafford.com
or email orders@trafford.com

Most Trafford titles are also available at major online book retailers.

Printed in the United States of America.

ISBN: 978-1-4669-5343-7 (sc)
ISBN: 978-1-4669-5342-0 (e)

Trafford rev. 08/16/2012

www.trafford.com

North America & international
toll-free: 1 888 232 4444 (USA & Canada)
phone: 250 383 6864 ♦ fax: 812 355 4082

# ABOUT THE STORY

Sophie was a girl born into a society that saw nothing wrong with divorce or war. She had had to have a hard life, first her life was ruined by her dad going to war. Then her evil stepmother tortured her that was when Sophie ran away. She had to face this time; life's torture of

homelessness and the fear of

losing her dad. She did find a

second home though, would

things ever be the same again . . .

# DEDICATION

I would like to dedicate this story to my sweet mum, Alice Addo-Yeboah, on the occasion of her 50th birthday, 21ST April, 2012. Mum I love you and I HOPE to have YOU always AROUND.

# ABOUT THE AUTHOR

Siobhan is an eleven year old girl who likes to always try to do something new. She likes to try different things like playing violin, guitar, recording and lots more. This story just happened to one of her new things that she decided to write about.

She lives in Hemel Hempstead, UK with her parents Mr and Mrs Reverend Pastor Addo-Yeboah. She has three brothers, Sam, Alex and Andrew, three sisters, Denisia, Leticia and Deborah.

# CHAPTER ONE

Sophie had a wonderful life. She lived with her dad, Conner, in a huge house almost like a mansion. Conner always had a plan or surprise for her which she always deserved. He had always treated Sophie the best. She meant the whole world to him and Sophie loved him as much as he loved her. She was also a Christian, she was very religious, and Sophie attended the local Church every Sunday and people we genuinely impressed of her wonderful achievement in her faith. Sophie had been the best student in the class. Some people called her goody two shoe but she didn't mind because she was allowed to do fun stuff like experiments and role-plays. Every evening Sophie's dad would take her for some ice cream, and would often tell her how proud he was of her.

## **But then this happened.**

One evening, Conner was taken away by force to fight in a war in a far-off land. That left his daughter with his evil wife,

Michelle, who was Sophie's step-mother. Sophie was only eight years old when her parents divorced and was left in care of the poor dad. Conner immediately married Michelle and boasted a lot that Michelle was a better woman who could be more tenderly caring, to raise Sophie in a sweet home full of love and peace. Michelle too pretended her love for him;

anytime Conner was around she

was the holiest angel for a step

mother. But because Conner

feared he would be forced to

join the army in the war if he

left his house he stayed around

and for one full year Sophie was

surrounded by joy.

How Michelle wished always

for her husband to be out of

sight. She would show Sophie

how much she wished her dead.

Sophie was either too beautiful for her liking or her children who would be born to be younger than Sophie would not be loved by their dad more like her. She promised to make Sophie's life a living hell. **The torture had just begun . . . . . . . . . .**

# CHAPTER TWO

Michelle was jealous of Sophie,

no doubt about that, but now

Conner was gone, Sophie was in the hands of a wicked stepmother. First, Michelle told Sophie to clean the whole house; she should do it or she would regret it, while she just sat there making more mess.

Sophie did it although she didn't want to. So in order to make her more miserable, Michelle got a whip and hit Sophie until she was bleeding. Sophie wailed and prayed to God to save her but Michelle just laughed and said; "God, he is not even real, besides nobody can." The next evening Sophie decided to run away, she packed all of her things and set off.

She wandered in the streets, darkness all over as she looked around for where she can get to stay. She had twisted her ankle, grazed her knee, majorly scraped her head and fell to the ground.

She screamed in anxiety but

nobody heard her.

That was the end of her! Or was

it . . .


After a while a young couple

came only to find a poor girl

lying on the ground, they

immediately dialled 999.

Fifteen minutes later she woke up only to find a plaster cast on her leg and a bandage around her head.

"What happened?" asked Sophie in amazement "Where am I?"

"We found you on the road" said the couple.

"Thank you", Sophie said looking around the room, "if you don't mind me saying? What are your names"?

"My name is Tillie" said the

woman in a soft voice.

"And my name is John" said the

man in a less so soft voice.

"Where do you live darling?" said

Tillie.

"Nowhere" wailed Sophie as she

burst into tears.

"That's ok" said Tillie "we will

take care of you"

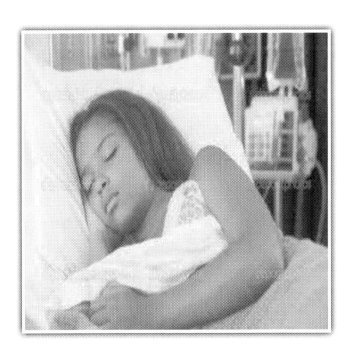

# CHAPTER THREE

"I'm so sorry to keep on disturbing you but can you look at my back. It feels really sore."

said Sophie

"Ok let's take a look" said Tillie

Tillie lifted Sophie's top and in amazement after a few seconds she finally said;

"How did you get all of these marks, Sophie?"

"My . . . my . . . .

my . . . stepmother had got a whip and hit me until I was bleeding" Sophie replied

"Where does she live, I need to report her to the police for your own safety and others."

"She . . . . She lives at 26 Maybore Square" said Sophie shyly.

"I'm calling the police right now. Now I know why we found you on the road, I thought something horrible happened to you"

So Tillie went to report to the police. The police found Michelle and took her to court and she ended in prison.

# CHAPTER FOUR

Two Months Later Sophie

went to her new home.

One early morning, a little young

boy came to Sophie's new house

to give her a letter

"Thank you" said Sophie in a

very generous mood.

Sophie opened the letter and in big bold letters it read:

**YOUR FATHER IS DEAD**

**SORRY FOR YOUR**

**LOSS**

*-THE ARMY*

Sophie wept and wept and did not eat or drink for almost fifteen days; her foster parents and other people around the neighbourhood began to worry.

# CHAPTER FIVE

My life is ruined, I have no real family, Sophie thought as she clambered down the stairs.

"Sophie, why do you look so disconsolate" Tillie asked

"My dad is dead; my step mums hates me and . . . wait a minute my blood related mum, she is still alive but I am not sure if I should ever stay with her. Can I borrow your phone, please", Sophie begged.

"Anything for you darling", but Tillie wanted to know,

"Thank you Tillie" said Sophie eagerly

Sophie dialled her mum's number and the phone began to ring, Sophie got so excited.

"Hello mum" Sophie said

"Hello Sophie" said Sheena (Sophie's mum) "Are you ok, Sophie"

"Yes mum, are you ok?"

"Yes darling . . . so is your father ok?" said Sheena

"No" replied Sophie

"Why?" asked Sheena

"I don't really ever want to talk about it" said Sophie

"Do you want to stay at mine for a while darling" said Sheena "Yes please mum but you will have to take real care for me because I have broken my leg and had recently had a mild concussion" said Sophie.

From that sweet phone conversation you would say what a lovely mum, but then why the divorce? Why would she leave a small girl to her own fate, in this wicked world?

# CHAPTER SIX

Sheena collected Sophie

the next day. Sophie was so

excited that she did not want

to remember why her parents

divorced.

At first Sheena had been looking

after Sophie but after a while

Sheena had just been going to

night club getting drunk. It was

like she didn't even care. Sophie

didn't know what was going to

happen next.

Sophie just thought it was just

the one off but it started to

become a problem. Instead of Sheena looking after Sophie, Sophie was looking after Sheena because she was binge drinking all the time. Sheena tells her she took to drinking after the divorce and now she cannot help it. Sophie realised it would be better to be a foster-child than a spoilt little mummy's girl. She called Tillie and John to take her back.

Tillie and John came to collect her A.S.A.P (As soon as possible).

# CHAPTER SEVEN

The following day Sophie went
to a new school. Everyone
wanted to play with her. From
then on, every day Sophie
would come home do all of
her homework then she would
ask to go outside and play for
a while. She had no problem

finding people to play with. She lived a happy life.

After 3 months Sophie got her plaster cast removed. She was over the moon; she had loved living with her new foster parents. She had a funeral for her dad. There were lots of tears but what do you expect, it's a funeral.

-THE END.

*In the beginning, God created the heavens and the earth.*

*The earth was void and there was darkness in the surface of the deep. The spirit of God moved over the surface of the water*

*For the wedges of sin is death but the gift of God is eternal.*

*Sophie's favourite Bible scripture for which she kept within her heart though her tough trails and toils.*

Printed in the United States
By Bookmasters